For Cathy,
may you continue to
inspire young minds!

FRANNIE AND PICKLES

by

Preston McClear

ILLUSTRATIONS

by

Nicholas Dollak

12-6-06

FIFTH PRINTING

© 2004 by Malibu Books For Children

Published in the United States of America by Malibu Books for Children,
a division of Malibu Films, Inc.

48 Broad Street, #134
Red Bank, N.J. 07701
Website: http://www.MalibuBooks.com
email: MalibuInc@aol.com

Printed in Hong Kong

10 9 8 7 6

ISBN: 1-929084-13-7

LCCN

MALIBU BOOKS
FOR CHILDREN

Jacket and book design by Nicholas Dollak

To Dean Jones

--- Preston McClear

For Holli-Joi and Thomas Martin,
two great kids

--- Uncle Nick

FRANNIE AND PICKLES

Frannie and Pickles did everything together.
Frannie loved being with Pickles most
out of her many friends.

Every morning Frannie made Pickles' breakfast.

They went bicycle riding later on.

©2003 N.Dollak

If it rained they played dress-up instead.

In the afternoon they liked to sit with
a cup of tea.

When evening came. Frannie would read
Pickles a story and then tuck him
into bed.

Frannie liked it best when she sat in
front of the fireplace with Pickles
curled up in her lap.

One day Frannie and Pickles were
having tea. Frannie said, "Pickles,
darling, I sure do feel odd."

Frannie lapped up the rest of her tea.

The next day Frannie and Pickles went for a walk. Frannie definitely felt out of sorts. "Whatever am I doing in the grass?" Frannie thought to herself as she sniffed a rose bush.

©2003 N. Dollak

During the trip to the grocery store
Frannie felt the worst yet. Frannie
barely even noticed she wasn't
driving.

When Frannie looked in the mirror
she had a beard.

"Pickles," said Frannie. "Me and you
been friends so long now We look just
like each other."

Pickles gave Frannie a terrific shave.

©2003 N. Dollak

The next day Frannie helped Pickles
chase the cat next door up her favorite
Ginkgo tree.

©2003 N. Dollak.

The mail man could hardly tell them
apart when they charged out the front
door to meet him.   Frannie and Pickles
were delighted.

They spent the afternoon trying different things.   Pickles beat Frannie at bridge.

Frannie beat Pickles at fetching the
frisbee.

WATERMELON
HALL

ARSINOITHERIUM
EARLY OLIGOCENE
AFRICA

AMARGASAURUS
ceous – S.AMERICA

©2003 N.Dollak

When evening came, Frannie was so
exhausted that she curled up in bed
while Pickles sat reading her a story.
Frannie drifted happily off to sleep thinking that
good friends do come in all shapes
and sizes.

THE END

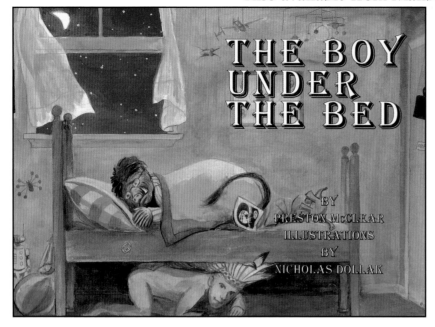